STORYTIME CLASSICS

The Secret Garden

by Frances Hodgson Burnett

retold by Janet Allison Brown • illustrated by Graham Rust

Puffin Books

PUFFIN BOOKS
Published by the Penguin Group
Penguin Putnam Books for Young Readers, 345 Hudson Street, New York, New York 10014, U.S.A.
Penguin Books Ltd, 27 Wrights Lane, London W8 5TZ, England
Penguin Books Australia Ltd, Ringwood, Victoria, Australia
Penguin Books Canada Ltd, 10 Alcorn Avenue, Toronto, Ontario, Canada M4V 3B2
Penguin Books (N.Z.) Ltd, 182-190 Wairau Road, Auckland 10, New Zealand

Penguin Books Ltd, Registered Offices: Harmondsworth, Middlesex, England

First published in Great Britain by Breslich & Foss, 2001
Published simultaneously by Viking and Puffin Books,
divisions of Penguin Putnam Books for Young Readers, 2001

10 9 8 7 6 5 4 3 2 1

Volume copyright © Breslich & Foss, 2001
Illustrations copyright © Graham Rust, 1986
Designed by Brian Wall
All rights reserved

LIBRARY OF CONGRESS CATALOGING-IN-PUBLICATION DATA
Brown, Janet Allison.
The secret garden / by Frances Hodgson Burnett ; illustrated by Graham
Rust ; re-told by Janet Allison Brown.
p.   cm.
Summary: A simplified retelling of ten-year-old Mary coming to live in a
lonely house on the Yorkshire moors and discovering an invalid cousin
and the mysteries of a locked garden.
ISBN 0-670-89911-9 (hardcover) — ISBN 0-14-131201-7 (pbk.)
[1. Orphans—Fiction. 2. Gardens—Fiction. 3. Physically
handicapped—Fiction. 4. Yorkshire (England)—Fiction.
5. England—Fiction.] I. Rust, Graham, ill. II. Burnett, Frances Hodgson,
1849–1924. Secret garden. III. Title.
PZ7.B814185 Se 2001   [E]—dc21   00-011882

Printed in Belgium

Frances Hodgson Burnett
1849–1924

Frances Hodgson Burnett, who wrote this story, was born in England but went to live in America when she was sixteen. Three years later her first book was published, and she eventually wrote over forty novels, many of them for children. Her most famous books are *A Little Princess*, *The Secret Garden*, and *Little Lord Fauntleroy*.

Mary Lennox had lived all her life in India. She had been given everything she wanted, except the love and attention of her parents, so she was a lonely girl. When her parents died, there was no one to take care of her except her uncle, Mr. Craven, who lived far away in England.

And that is how she came to be riding in a carriage over the wild Yorkshire moors, and into the courtyard of Misselthwaite Manor.

Mr. Craven was very rich, but very sad. His wife had died many years before, and he spent his time traveling. He didn't want to see Mary, so he left her to the housekeeper, Mrs. Medlock.

Mary was taken upstairs and down a long corridor. "Here you are," said Mrs. Medlock. "This room and the next are where you'll live— and you must keep to them. Don't forget that!"

With that, Mrs. Medlock swept away, leaving Mary alone staring out at the moors.

The next morning when Mary awoke, Martha, the housemaid, was making a fire.

In India, Mary had maids who dressed her and did everything she told them to do. Here, things were very different. "It's time you learned to do things for yourself," said Martha.

Martha chatted to Mary about her family, who lived on the moors, and about her brother Dickon, who loved animals.

And she told Mary a strange secret about Misselthwaite Manor: "One of the gardens is locked up," she said. "No one has been in it for ten years!"

There was not much to do in the house, so
Mary spent most of her time in the gardens.
She was used to playing alone. She went down
lots of paths, and found fruit trees, and walls
with doors in them, and a patch of winter
vegetables. She met Ben Weatherstaff, the old
gardener, and made friends with a perky,
clever little robin.

She did not find the secret garden—but she
began to wonder where it might be.

One day, she saw something half buried in a flower bed. She picked it up—it was a key! "Perhaps it is the key to the garden," she said in a whisper.

Suddenly her friend the robin flew to a wall and began to sing. There, under the ivy, was a door she had not seen before.

Mary put the key in the lock, and turned it.

Mary pushed open the door and found herself standing inside the secret garden. It was the most mysterious looking place anyone could imagine.

"How still it is!" she whispered. She felt as if she had found a world all her own.

As the days went by, Mary spent as much time as she could in the garden, pulling out weeds and enjoying her special secret. One day, she heard a low whistle. She went out to see what it was.

A boy was sitting under a tree playing a rough wooden pipe. He had very blue eyes and rosy cheeks. A brown squirrel watched him from the tree, a pheasant and two rabbits sat close by listening, and a crow perched on his shoulder.

It was Martha's brother Dickon.

Dickon was friendly and gentle, and before long, Mary was showing him her garden. Dickon knew all about animals and plants. He showed Mary how to tell which roses were alive and which were dead. He showed her how to clear away weeds and stir the earth to let the air in.

"This is the best fun I ever had in my life—waking up a garden," said Dickon.

That night, when Mary was lying in bed, she thought she heard someone crying.

She got up and followed the voice down one of the forbidden corridors where she had never been before. She pushed open a door and found herself in a big bedroom. In the bed was a boy.

"Are you a ghost?" he whispered.

"No," said Mary. "Are you?"

"No," he replied. "I'm Colin."

Colin was Mr. Craven's son. He had been ill all his life, and couldn't stand or walk. He didn't like people to stare at him, so he stayed in his room all the time. When Colin didn't get his own way, he screamed until the servants gave him whatever he wanted.

But Mary knew exactly how to deal with Colin—because in India she had behaved in exactly the same way! When Colin screamed, she ignored him.

Soon Colin discovered that it was more fun to be friends with Mary than to be miserable. And once he realized this, he started to get better.

Colin wanted to meet Dickon as well. The servants were astonished when he told them, "A boy, and a fox, and a crow, and two squirrels, and a newborn lamb are coming to see me this morning. I want them brought upstairs as soon as they come!"

Dickon and the animals arrived, and they all sat down to plan how they could get Colin out of the house and into the secret garden without anyone seeing them.

First, they carried Colin downstairs and put him into a wheelchair. Then Dickon wheeled him into the garden, and Colin told all the servants except for Ben Weatherstaff to stay away.

Everything was new to Colin. He looked at the sky and smelled the breeze and listened to the birds singing. Dickon and Mary wheeled him all around the garden—and at last they took him to the secret garden. He stared at everything—the roses and the trees and the walls.

"I shall get well!" he cried.

Every day, Colin did exercises to make his legs strong. One day when he felt especially well, he and the others sat under a tree and began to wish very hard for Colin to be able to walk. Slowly Colin stood up.

"You can do it! You can do it!" said Mary. "I tell you, you can!"

Then while they all wished even harder, Colin took an unsteady step forward and began to walk for the first time in his life. "Look at me!" he cried. "I did it!"